The Show that Smells

Also by Derek McCormack

Grab Bag

The Haunted Hillbilly

The Show that Smells

Derek McCormack

For Lynn —

With affection and admiration and oodles of ghoulish glamour!

Love,
Derek

O)))) ← sequins

ECW Press

MISFIT

Published by ECW Press
2120 Queen Street East, Suite 200,
Toronto, Ontario M4E 1E2
416.694.3348 / info@ecwpress.com

LIBRARY AND ARCHIVES CANADA CATALOGUING IN PUBLICATION

McCormack, Derek
The show that smells / Derek McCormack.
ISBN: 978-1-55022-855-7
I. Title.
PS8575.C664S56 2008 C813'.54 C2008-902382-X

The publication of *The Show that Smells* has been generously supported by the Canada Council for the Arts, which last year invested $20.1 million in writing and publishing throughout Canada, by the Ontario Arts Council, by the Government of Ontario through Ontario Book Publishing Tax Credit, by the OMDC Book Fund, an initiative of the Ontario Media Development Corporation, and by the Government of Canada through the Book Publishing Industry Development Program (BPIDP).

Canada Council for the Arts Conseil des Arts du Canada Canadä ONTARIO ARTS COUNCIL CONSEIL DES ARTS DE L'ONTARIO

Printing: Coach House Printing

This book is set in Tribute and Arial

Sections of *The Show that Smells* appeared in or will appear in *Taddle Creek* magazine and *MYTHTYM*. The author acknowledges the generous support of the Writers' Reserve Program of the Ontario Arts Council.

PRINTED AND BOUND IN CANADA

ECW PRESS
ecwpress.com

~~Angst @~~ Angst @ Type, Oct 20/08, Derek very funny + sweet.

☆ Fucker

Please!

Fuck You

Tru too 1/2

PIG

The author thanks Howard Akler, Nathalie Atkinson, ~~Tony Burgess~~, Joey Comeau, ~~Kevin Connolly~~, Dennis Cooper, Trinie Dalton, ~~Jack David~~, Hadley Dyer, Vincent Fecteau, Grant Heaps, ~~Michael Holmes~~, Johanna Ingalls, Meaghan Kent, Susan Kernohan, Kevin Killian, David Livingstone, Guy Maddin, Jason McBride, Cynthia McCormack, Melissa McCormack, Murray McCormack, Casey McKinney, Hilary McMahon, Richard Eoin Nash, Christopher Paulin, Ian Phillips, Nen Reyes, Andrea Rosen, Daniel Sinker, ~~Ken Sparling~~, Adam Sternbergh, Johnny Temple, Conan Tobias, Christopher Waters, Greg Wells, Joel Westendorf, Alana Wilcox, and all at ECW Press and Akashic Books.

Asshole

JESUS CHRIST!

Special thanks to David Altmejd.

The first time I met him was in a bookstore, 18 years ago.

The Show that Smells

Cast of Characters

Jimmie Rodgers . . . Himself

Carrie Rodgers . . . Joan Crawford

The Reporter . . . Derek McCormack

The Carter Family . . . Themselves

Coco Chanel . . . Herself

Renfield . . . Lon Chaney

The Vogue Vampire . . . ?

Story by

Derek McCormack

Directed by

Tod Browning

1

Jimmie Rodgers.

Jimmie Rodgers. Jimmie Rodgers.

Jimmie Rodgers. Jimmie Rodgers. Jimmie Rodgers.

Jimmie Rodgers. Jimmie Rodgers. Jimmie Rodgers. Jimmie Rodgers. Jimmie Rodgers. Jimmie Rodgers. Jimmie Rodgers.

Jimmie Rodgers in a Mirror Maze.

Jimmie poses like he's shooting publicity. Blazer buttoned, blazer unbuttoned—he tries it both ways. Plumps his pocket puff. Picks lint from lapels.

"You're fine," he says.

"You look fine," he says.

"Everything's going to—" He coughs. "Everything's going to be—" Coughs up crap. *Splat*. On spats.

Jimmie Rodgers.

Carrie Rodgers. Jimmie Rodgers.

Carrie Rodgers. Jimmie Rodgers. Carrie Rodgers.

Jimmie Rodgers. Carrie Rodgers. Jimmie Rodgers. Carrie Rodgers. Jimmie Rodgers. Carrie Rodgers. Jimmie Rodgers.

Jimmie Rodgers and Carrie Rodgers in a Mirror Maze.

Carrie Rodgers winds her way through the Maze.

Jimmie's at a dead end. Doubled up.

"Darling, no." She sinks down beside him. His sleeve's sopping. Sputum. It will dry stiffer than starch. "The carnival is killing you," she says. "You have to leave." Sputum smells like socks. From her purse she pulls out a bottle.

He sticks the neck up his nose. *Chanel N°5*.

"Never," he says.

"Look at yourself," Carrie says.

"I'm fine." Jimmie sniffs *Chanel N°5*. He spits. Sputum. Smells like Saks.

"You're thin. You're pale." So's she. She's supposed to be.

Her suit is Chanel. Spring show. "You should go back to the sanitarium."

"So they can what—slice me up? Stick me with needles? Shut me in a room to rot?" He pours perfume on his sleeve. "I'm Jimmie Rodgers! The carnival singer! Who would I be if I stopped singing?" He hacks. "Nobody. Nothing."

"A carnival is not a cure!" she says. "*Chanel Nº5* is not a cure!"

Jimmie Rodgers.

Carrie Rodgers. Jimmie Rodgers.

Carrie Rodgers. Jimmie Rodgers. Carrie Rodgers.

Jimmie Rodgers. Carrie Rodgers. Jimmie Rodgers. Carrie Rodgers. Jimmie Rodgers. Carrie Rodgers. Jimmie Rodgers.

Jimmie Rodgers and Carrie Rodgers and me in a Mirror Maze.

"Jumping Jehoshophat!" Jimmie jumps.

"Where did you come from?" Carrie says.

"Paris," I say.

"The mirrors!" Carrie says.

"You're not there!" Jimmie says.

"I'm a vampire," I say. "I write for *Vampire Vogue*, the style bible of the fashionable fiend."

"There's *Vogue* for vampires?" she says.

"We wear clothes," I say. "We're not werewolves."

"Stay away, devil," Jimmie says, "or I swear I'll—" *Cough*.

"I haven't come to kill you," I say. "I've come to write about you." In mirrors, I look like nothing. I look like lamé. "A carnival, a singing star, his lady—why would Elsa Schiaparelli summon me to such a place?"

"*The* Elsa Schiaparelli?" Carrie says.

"The Vogue Vampire," I say. "The Dracula of Dressmaking."

"She makes clothes for movie stars!" she says. "She's famous!"

"Famously fiendish!" I say. "Fashion is her feint. A demon who dresses well-heeled women around the world. She makes them look beautiful. She makes them smell beautiful. Then she eats them."

Jimmie Rodgers.

Carrie Rodgers. Jimmie Rodgers.

Carrie Rodgers. Jimmie Rodgers. Carrie Rodgers.

Jimmie Rodgers. Carrie Rodgers. Jimmie Rodgers. Carrie

Rodgers. Jimmie Rodgers. Carrie Rodgers. Jimmie Rodgers. Carrie Rodgers.

Jimmie Rodgers and Carrie Rodgers and Elsa Schiaparelli and me in a Mirror Maze. Elsa Lanchester plays Elsa Schiaparelli. There's a resemblance.

"Am I late?" Schiaparelli asks.

"Fashionably." I kiss her hand. "You smell divine."

"I am divine." She fans herself. "The latest fragrance from *Maison de Schiaparelli*. I call it *Shocking!*—as in freak shows—shocking and amazing!"

Jimmie and Carrie act scared.

"How do I look?" Schiaparelli's dress is orange, yellow, and pink. Mostly pink. Sleeves sparkle. Sequins are celluloid. "I cut it from sideshow banners. 'Valentines,' freaks call them. Isn't that quaint?

"I learned this from my new assistant—Mr. Renfield. He's a geek. He beheads rats. He bites them!" Scuttling along the corridor behind her: Lon Chaney. White skin, white eyes. Hair? Detergent would be jealous. Blood crusted on his chin. Rat fur stuck to his teeth. Looks like decay.

"He has a way with accessories." Schiaparelli points to his suit. It's white. Was white. Bib of blood. Black flies embellish it. Fruit flies flit. Living lint.

"And it's not only him. The Fortune Teller's turban! The Witch Doctor's skull stick! The Ubangi's lip plate! The Snake Lady—her anaconda is a boa! The Alligator Man—what a purse he would make!

"Freak fashion. Geek chic. It inspired my new haute couture collection for humans—the Carnival Collection! Soon Schiaparelli clients will dress like the Half-Man, Half-Woman and the Mule-Faced Lady. Ostrich girls in ostrich plumes. Lobster ladies in lobster gowns.

"It's like I always say: Clothes make the inhuman."

"Women won't wear freak clothes," Carrie says.

"Women wear what I tell them to wear," Schiaparelli says.

"When all the world's well-dressed women are dressed and perfumed like freaks," Schiaparelli says, "I will make them freaks—in a carnival, a vampire carnival—a carnival of fashion and death!" She changes. Fangs flower. Pupils as pink paillettes. "And freaks are only part of the fun!

"Men will be rides.

"Women will be games.

"Children will be snacks."

Schiaparelli's face is a special effect.

"What would a carnival be without a tent show?" Schiaparelli says. "Jimmie Rodgers, the Midway Minstrel, America's Carnival Crooner—I want you to sing at the carnival to end all carnivals."

"Why would I?" Jimmie asks.

"You're ill, Mr. Rodgers," Schiaparelli says, "ill with tuberculosis. I know this, I have heard your record— 'TB Blues.' Catchy. But I am stronger than TB. I will drain you of blood. Without blood, the disease will die. I will feed you my blood. And you will live forever—singing!"

"Go to hell," Jimmie says.

"Mr. Rodgers," Schiaparelli says, "you will sing for me whether you want to or not. You will sing for your supper—and you'll be supper!

"Renfield! See that he's comfortably imprisoned." She

points a pink fingernail. A pink dinner ring. Dazzles. Pink, pink, pink! "And bring Mrs. Rodgers as well. She's comely, yes? She will star in my sideshow."

"I'd rather die!" Carrie says.

"You don't say," Schiaparelli says. "Then I shall put you on the midway. Slit you open. Twist your intestines into animal shapes. When you rot, you'll give off gas, your insides will inflate. Abracadabra—animal balloons!

"I shall drag the midway with you. Do you know what that means? I will stick a meat hook in you, then lug your bleeding, barely breathing body through the sawdust to the wild animal show. The animals will go wild when they smell you coming. The audience will go wild when they smell you, too.

"I shall put you in the animal show. Do you like animals? Lions, tigers, hyenas—and you! They will snap your neck, then eat your meat, your bones, your brain. Carrie carrion. You'll be dinner, then droppings. Do you know what carnies call an animal show? The Show that Smells!"

"A sensational name," I say.

Jimmie Rodgers.

Carrie Rodgers. Jimmie Rodgers.

Carrie Rodgers. Jimmie Rodgers. Cornered.

Lon Chaney closes in. Nosferatu nails.

"Stay away, you fiend," Jimmie says, "or I swear I'll—" A cough cuts him off. "I'll—" He takes a fit. Falls to the floor.

"Leave him alone!" Carrie's pink with panic. Perfume floats from her throat, wrists, soft spots in her elbows. Where blood abounds. It rises from Jimmie. A screen of scent. Screen or scream?

"Aaarrrgghhhhh!" Chaney says. "*Chanel N°5!*" Worse than wolfsbane. Gruesomer than garlic. Chaney clutches his throat like he's strangling himself. All vampires act like silent stars.

Cowering, cringing, crying—Chaney acts like an actress.

"You're afraid of perfume?" Carrie lords the bottle over him. She drips a drop onto him. It burns like battery acid. Blended with bleach. Skin smokes. Seared hair. Seared skin. Seared seersucker. Stinks. *Chaney N°5.*

"It's been blessed!" I say. Anointed perfume. Holy eau de toilette.

"Chanel sanctifies her scents!" Schiaparelli says. "She thinks she can protect her clients from me! She can't! No one can!"

"We'll see about that!" Carrie splashes Chaney. An ounce costs. He screeches in close-up. He's a master at makeup. His forehead flames. His forehead was frog skin. His nose—mortician's wax. It drips down his lips. His jaw drops. Off. The things he does with gutta-percha! He hurls himself at a mirror. Smashes through. Splinters stick. He bleeds. Borrowed blood. It's brown syrup. Brown looks red in black-and-white.

"Chanel can't keep you alive forever!" Schiaparelli floats up off the floorboards. André Perugia designed her shoes.

"Your perfume will fade!" she says, suspended like a chandelier. A chandelier in a Mirror Maze? It's overkill!

"Your perfume will die! Your perfume will sell out or be discontinued!" Sequins! She shines chandelierically. The Maze shot through with thirteen shades of white light. "Mark my words, Madame, the moment you find yourself without *Chanel N°5*—"

She makes herself into mist. Vampires, like perfumes, vaporize.

"I will have you on the cover of *Vampire Vogue*," I say to Carrie. "Circulation will soar. Madame Schiaparelli always sells magazines—her fans are fans forever—undead couture clients never die!"

I vanish. It's done with mirrors.

Jimmie's flat on the floor. Carrie crouches, comforts him, coos to him, his head in her lap.

"Hush," she says.

"The vampire's gone," she says.

"Here comes the Carter Family," she says.

Jimmie Rodgers.

Carrie Rodgers. Mother Maybelle Carter.

Sara Carter. A.P. Carter. Jimmie Rodgers.

Carrie Rodgers. Mother Maybelle Carter. Sara Carter. A.P. Carter. Jimmie Rodgers. Carrie Rodgers. Mother Maybelle Carter. Sara Carter. A.P. Carter.

Jimmie Rodgers and Carrie Rodgers and Mother Maybelle and Sara and A.P.—the Carter Family—in a Mirror Maze.

"Fangs?" Maybelle says.

"Fancy clothes?" she says.

"Fancy haircuts?" she says.

"Yes, yes, yes," Carrie says. "How did you know?"

“We’re the Carter Family,” Maybelle says. “Down-home singers by day, vampire killers by night!” She cocks her arm like a choir conductor. Carters start to sing. A signature song—“Keep on the Sunny Side.”

“Vampires love clothes,” Maybelle says. “Vampires love carnivals. Folks dolled up, parading down the midway, flirting in the Funhouse, fornicating on the Ferris wheel—pardon my French!

“Vampires smell vanity!” she says. “Vampires smell sin!” The Carter Family is not camera-friendly. Sara’s squat. A.P.’s a tent pole. Maybelle’s built like Marie Dressler. She’s gray beyond her years. The reverse of vampires. And movie stars.

“We sing our hymns in the opry.” *Rag opry* is carny slang for a tent show. “We sing, then we—”

“Stake!” A.P. says. “I see a vampire, I stab him in the heart!”

“You see a vampire, you poop your pants,” Maybelle says.

Sara’s silent. “That’s true,” she says.

“This is your fault, Jimmie!” Mother Maybelle says. “You stand in here, preening and primping—it’s not natural! It’s not right!”

"Amen!" Sara says.

"I don't always poop my pants," A.P. says.

"Stop sulking!" Maybelle swats him.

"You're not being fair, Maybelle," Carrie says. "Jimmie never asked for any of this. Look at him, he's—"

"You're just as bad, Miss Carrie! French clothes and French jewelry and French perfume." Maybelle's dress is homemade. Worn out by washboards. Sara's in hand-me-down hose. Runs darned, darned, and darned again. They bulge like varicose veins. A.P.'s suit is second-hand. It shows. "You've got Jimmie dressed up like some kewpie doll," Maybelle says, "smelling like a whore! There's no place for fashion in country music!"

Jimmie: Coughs. Coughs. Coughs. Coughs. Coughs. Barfs blood. Blood doesn't come out of clothes.

2

i.

Carrie Rodgers.

Carrie Rodgers. Carrie Rodgers.

Carrie Rodgers. Carrie Rodgers. Carrie Rodgers.

Carrie Rodgers. Carrie Rodgers. Carrie Rodgers. Carrie Rodgers. Carrie Rodgers. Carrie Rodgers. Carrie Rodgers.

Carrie Rodgers comes to me in a Mirror Maze.

"Déjà vu!" I say.

"Where is Mrs. Schiaparelli?" she says.

"She'll be here shortly," I say. "She's flying in from France."

V.

Carrie Rodgers. V.

Carrie Rodgers. V. Carrie Rodgers.

V. Carrie Rodgers. V. Carrie Rodgers. V. Carrie Rodgers. V. Carrie Rodgers. V. Carrie Rodgers. V. Carrie Rodgers. V.

Carrie Rodgers and a bat and me in a Mirror Maze. The bat becomes Schiaparelli. Her blouse is batwinged. Becoming!

"*Chérie!*" Schiaparelli says.

Carrie pulls perfume from her pocket.

Patch pocket. The suit's Chanel. The perfume: *Chanel N°5*.

"Come to kill me?" Schiaparelli says. "You'll need more than an ounce of that skunky spray. I'm a tough old bat."

"I didn't come to kill you," Carrie says. "*Chanel N°5*—my husband loves it. He sniffs it before breakfast. He sniffs it before bed. He sniffs it before shows." Tears menace mascara. "He can't smell it anymore."

"Better sick than Chanel," Schiaparelli says.

"*Le bon mot*," I say.

"*Le bon mort*," Schiaparelli says.

"It's not only *Chanel N°5*." Carrie empties out her pockets.

My Sin by Jeanne Lanvin. "I wore that on my wedding night." *Temptation* by Madeleine Vionnet. "Our one-year anniversary." *Jicky* by Guerlain. "Valentine's Day." *Joy* by Jean Patou. "Jimmie bought this for my birthday." *Dans la Nuit* by Charles Frederick Worth—a black bottle in a black box. Satinwood, tailored with black satin. Comfortable as a casket.

"Chanel is swill," Schiaparelli says.

"Charles Frederick Worth—worthless," she says.

"Your husband is lucky that Patou is lost on him," she says. "Patou? Pee-ew! *Jicky?* Icky!"

"Prince Matchabelli?" I say.

"Prince Smelly!" Schiaparelli says.

"Jimmie is dying!" Carrie says. "All he smells is blood. And sputum. And pus. He smells his lungs. They smell like bowels. His breath is so bad!" Carrie clutches Schiaparelli's collar. "You have powers. You have perfumes. Make him a scent to kill the smell. Make him a scent to make him well."

"What would the bottle look like?" Schiaparelli says. "What would the label look like? What would we call it—*Eau de Yodel?*

"What family would his perfume belong to?" she says, circling Carrie. "Would it be an earthy Chypre? A spicy Oriental? A ferny Fougère? Something bold, or bashful? Best seller, or best smeller?

"The heart note—vetiver or vanilla? Wormwood or worm food? Tuberose or tuberculosis? A million roses must die to distill a drop *de l'esprit*." She strokes Carrie's cheek. Vampires, like perfumes, are room temperature. "What would it be worth to you, Madame Rodgers? What price would you pay?"

Mother Maybelle Carter.

Sara Carter. A.P. Carter.

Carrie Rodgers. Mother Maybelle Carter. Sara Carter.

A.P. Carter. Carrie Rodgers. Mother Maybelle Carter. Sara Carter. A.P. Carter. Carrie Rodgers. Mother Maybelle Carter. Sara Carter. A.P. Carter.

Carrie Rodgers and the Carter Family and Elsa Schiaparelli and me in a Mirror Maze.

"The Carter Family!" Maybelle says.

"Christian soldiers for Christ!" Sara says.

"I think I forgot something in the Ford," A.P. says, turning tail.

Maybelle stops him. Swats him.

"Cartier?" Schiaparelli says.

"Carter," I say. "Hillbilly Van Helsings."

"We put the sing in Van Helsing!" Maybelle says. "We'll put the fear of God in you!" She starts into a traditional tune—"Sunshine in the Shadows."

"This is singing?" I say.

"Caterwauling," Schiaparelli says. "Carter-wauling."

"Ha!"

"Ha! Ha!"

"Ha! Ha! Ha!" Schiaparelli and I laugh in a Mirror Maze.

Maybelle stomps her shoe. "What's so darned funny!"

"Your hair!" Schiaparelli says. "Your clothes! You look like a family of scarecrows! Where do scarecrows shop? Marshall Field's?"

"Fashion fiends!" Maybelle says. "You should be afraid!"

"We are!" Schiaparelli says. "Afraid you'll sing again!"

"In the name of God, the Grand Old Party and the Grand Ole Opry!" Maybelle says. "Go back to France!" She tosses a grenade. It's not a grenade. It's a clove of garlic. Strapped to her shoulder—a bandolier of buds.

"Garlic?" Schiaparelli says, slinking toward her. Sara wears a corsage of wolfsbane. A.P. carries a sage smudge stick. It shakes like a conductor's baton. "I'm not Count Dracula, darlings—spices and stinkweed won't frighten me off!"

"She's gonna eat me!" A.P. says.

"True," she says. "Though there is one odor that could defeat me—*Chanel N°5*. Madame Rodgers is holding it in her hands."

"Carrie!" Maybelle says.

"Spray her with it!" Sara says.

"Don't let me die!" A.P. says. "Please!"

"I can't!" Carrie could cry. She cries on cue.

"I knew she wouldn't spray me," Schiaparelli says. "Madame Rodgers needs me to make a perfume for her. My price? Her soul—a soul for a scent!"

"I have no choice!" Carrie says. "Sniffing *Chanel N°5* hasn't helped Jimmie at all—and it's blessed by priests! Mrs. Schiaparelli swears she can cure him with her perfume. She swears." She sobs, surrenders her *Chanel N°5* to Schiaparelli. "A deal with the Devil—may God have mercy on my soul!"

Her soul is chiffon.

Soul. Blouse.

"TB is but a trifle!" Schiaparelli says, rising into the air. "I am TB; I am smallpox; I am the plague!"

"Sh-sh-she's floating!" A.P. flees. Slams into a glass wall. Falls.

"I am the death bed, the abattoir, the boneyard!" Schiaparelli says. Smoke swirls out from a smoke machine, hiding wires holding her. "I am the sewers of Paris, of London, of New York—*les fleurs du mal odeur!*"

"Sh-sh-she's talking French!" A.P. leaps up, dashes down a dead end. He slips on something. Feet fly up. His shoe size: EEE!

"*Chanel N°5?*" she says. "I am *Charnel N°5!*" Smoke is scenic. Studio smoke! Water, sugar, and glycerine. Smoke-colored. Smoke-shaped. It snakes through the Maze like it knows what it wants. Sara coughs. A.P. coughs. Maybelle collapses, coughing. "I am the deadliest force in fashion—and there's not a soul alive who can stop me!"

"I can," Coco Chanel says.

Smoke dies down.

Schiaparelli floats down to the floor.

"*Merde*," she says, rolling her eyes my way.

Coco Chanel.

Carrie Rodgers. Mother Maybelle.

Sara. A.P. Coco Chanel. Carrie Rodgers.

Mother Maybelle. Sara. A.P. Coco Chanel. Carrie Rodgers. Mother Maybelle. Sara. A.P. Coco Chanel. Carrie Rodgers. Mother Maybelle. Sara. A.P.

Coco Chanel and Carrie Rodgers and the Carter Family and Elsa Schiaparelli and me in a Mirror Maze.

"Who in the blue-belted blazes are you?" Maybelle says.

"I am Coco Chanel," Chanel says. "I have devoted my life to crafting comfortable, classy, Christian couture. Demure daywear. Demure evening wear. Demure costumes for the beach. I made sunbathing chic."

Coco Chanel plays and wears herself. A skirted suit of taupe tweed, or, as the French say, *le tweed*.

"We're the Carter Family!" Maybelle says. "We've devoted our life to singing and stabbing vampires!"

"We are soldiers in the same battle," Chanel says, spinning like a ballerina in a ballerina jewelry box. She shines. Cuffs armor her arms. Crosses adorn them. Byzantine. Russian. Greek. Embossed on her buttons—her logo, a C and a C. Back to back. Reflected. "You fight Schiaparelli for the souls of men. I fight Schiaparelli for the souls of clothes."

"Clothes don't have souls," Maybelle says.

"Clothes have linings," A.P. says.

"Schiaparelli, Schiaparelli, Schiaparelli," Chanel says to the Carters. "Couturiers whispered her name in terrified tones. She was a legend, a figure feared but seldom seen—a Satanic seamstress who catered to vampires.

"And then, not so many years ago, she stepped from the shadows," Chanel says. "She started creating clothes for human clients. Even the names of her collections curdled my Christian soul—the Pagan Collection, the Zodiac Collection!" She crosses herself.

"Gaud is her God!" Chanel says. "I saw grotesque Schiaparelli gowns in the pages of *Vogue*. I saw grotesque Schiaparelli gowns at the Opèra, at the Ritz. She'd steal my clients, then slaughter them. I devoted myself to destroying her. I am guarded in my mission by the archangel Gabriel, my namesake. 'Coco' is my nickname; my given name is 'Gabrielle.' 'Archangel' is an anagram for 'Chanel rag!'"

Schiaparelli swans toward Chanel.

"You look old," Schiaparelli says.

"You look evil," Chanel says.

Lon Chaney creeps up behind Chanel.

"A Mirror Maze?" Chanel's shoes stick. The floor is sticky. Pop. Puke. "It's tacky, even for you, Elsa."

"Mirror Maze?" Schiaparelli says. "Mirror *maison*. My *maison de couture*—a *maison* in a *maison* in a *maison* in a *maison* in a *maison* in a *maison* in a *maison* in a *maison* in a *maison* in a *maison* in a *maison* in a *maison* in a *maison* in a *maison!*"

Chaney creeps closer to Chanel. Maggots infest his face. Shimmering like sequins.

"Mirrors," Chanel says, "are hardly your hallmark. A mirrored staircase is the centerpiece of my *maison* on rue Cambon in Paris."

"*Au contraire*, Coco," Schiaparelli says. "The Mirror Maze

is my milieu. My smokescreen. A vampire Versailles. It could be crawling with vampires as we speak. You would never know. Until it was too late."

"Of course I would, Elsa," Chanel says. "I smell the rot." She spins, sprays Chaney. Perfume films his eyes. He sees sandalwood! He sees ylang-ylang! He sees Lily of the Valley! Chaney concocted the coating—collodion and egg white. She sprays again. He crumples like cloth in a cloud of *Chanel N°5*. He smells like number two. He drags himself down the corridor. Skin sizzling. Stop time. Blood is makeup.

"He needs a facial," I say.

"He needs a face," Schiaparelli says.

"Your perfume is powerful," Schiaparelli says. "So is mine." Brandishing a pink box: "*Voila!* The latest scent from Maison de Schiaparelli—*Shocking!*"

"Shocking how?" Chanel says.

"The name of it is *Shocking!*"

"How shocking could a name be?"

"*Shocking!* It's called *Shocking! Sacre bleu!*"

"Behold my bottle!" Schiaparelli says.

"Your bottle has breasts!" Chanel says.

"It's a Frenchie," Schiaparelli says. "Frenchie, Hula Honey, Sweater Girl, Apache Babe—these are kinds of kewpie dolls. All share a silhouette—Mae West. Kewpies are carnival prizes. Plaster of Paris. Painted. My doll is cut from crystal. The bottle's Baccarat." The doll's head comes off. A neck is a nozzle.

"Smell!" Schiaparelli sprays the air. Sprays herself. Perfume clings to dead skin. It smells pink. "The top note—sugar. Pink popcorn, pink cotton candy, pink bubble gum. The middle note—sawdust. Pink sawdust!"

"The bottom?" Chanel says.

"Blood!" Schiaparelli says, spraying. "The blood of little boys, the blood of little girls. A bead in every bottle." She sprays. "To the living, it's undetectable. To the undead, it's delectable." She sprays. "From miles away, we can smell it, we can follow it, we can find the women who wear it—the women who wear it, the men they're with—" She sprays Chanel. "And you!"

"Monster!" Maybelle says.

"Murderer!" Sara says.

"Mommy," A.P. says.

"Come, boy!" Schiaparelli says.

Down the corridor comes a dog.

"Coco, your *parfumeur* is Ernest Beaux—an inapt name if ever there was one," Schiaparelli says. "Meet my *parfumeur*—Jo-Jo, the Dog-Faced Boy."

Fur flourishes on his forehead, his eyelids, his lips. I shake his hand. Paw. Dead fleas fall into my palm. A circus's worth.

"A freak!" Chanel says.

"A diseased freak," Schiaparelli says. "He suffers from a syndrome! Hypertrichinosis. He's hairy as a Lab."

Jo-Jo whimpers. Jo-Jo licks his snout.

"All his life," Schiaparelli says, "he's been laughed at by the likes of you—ridiculed, rebuffed, and rejected. Me? I admire his remarkable gift—his sense of smell. He's a bloodhound—a born *parfumeur*."

Jo-Jo is a staple of sideshows. He plays himself in this picture. It's a vampire movie. Bit parts abound.

"He has a way with accessories." Schiaparelli points to his flea collar. A silver leash dangles off his neck.

"And it's not only him. The Fortune Teller's turban! The Witch Doctor's skull stick! The Ubangi's lip plate! The Snake Lady—her anaconda is a boa! The Alligator Man—what a purse he would make!

"Freak fashion. Geek chic. It inspired my new haute couture collection for humans—the Carnival Collection! Soon Schiaparelli clients will dress like the Half-Man, Half-Woman and the Mule-Faced Lady. Ostrich girls in ostrich plumes. Lobster ladies in lobster gowns.

"It's like I always say: Clothes make the inhuman."

"*Caveat emptor!*" I say.

"Cravat *emptor!*" Schiaparelli says.

"When all the world's well-dressed women are dressed and perfumed like freaks," Schiaparelli says, "I will make them freaks—in a carnival, a vampire carnival, a carnival of fashion and death!" She changes. Fangs flower. Pupils pink paillettes. "And freaks are only part of the fun!

"Men will be rides.

"Women will be games.

"Children will be snacks."

Schiaparelli's face is a special effect.

"My husband belongs in a tent show, not an oxygen tent," Carrie says. "I will wear your perfume, Mrs. Schiaparelli. I will be your freak."

Tears trickle down her cheeks.

Tears are eye drops.

"For you, *Shocking!*" Schiaparelli says, showering Carrie. "For your husband, *Shocking!*—but with a twist. Watch as I transform perfume into prescription. *Monsieur!*"

I become a bat. Sit on her shoulder.

She plucks me up. Squeezes me.

I shit into *Shocking!*

"Bat feces—rich in saltpeter. As he inhales, Jimmie's lungs will absorb it. It will leech into his bloodstream, cleansing corpuscles, obliterating bacteria." She squeezes. I pee. A bat's bladder is not big. "Bat urine—it will crystallize in his lungs as it cools, shrinking infected tissue. Stopping sputum from spreading."

"This isn't science!" Chanel says. "It's specious!"

"Propagation of the specious!" Schiaparelli says.

"Perfume is life!" Schiaparelli says. "Perfume is death! I am perfume itself—life and death distilled. *Flacon de vie—parfum du parfum!*"

"Squeak, squeak, squeak!" I say.

"Life," she says of *Shocking!* "Take it to the Sanitarium, Madame Rodgers. Take it to your husband. Douse his bedsheets. Douse his bathrobe. Douse his bedpan. When he is well, you will return to me."

Carrie takes it. Exits.

"Death," she says, holding Carrie's *Chanel N°5*. "You will die, Coco. You will die, Carter Family." She strokes the crystal bottle. Summoning something. A speck. A black speck. Flapping inside the flaçon.

A bat. Another appears. Another, and another. *Chanel N°V. Chanel N°VV. Chanel N°VVV.* Base note, heart note, top note—bat. What did the vampire plop into her bath? Bat beads. She unstops the bottle and *boom!*—bats burst out, blazing through the Maze. Stab bats? Maybelle ducks down. Bats besiege her. Bats as bow ties. Bats as barrettes. Bats dream of being bandeaux. The sound!—Foley artists flapping. Leather gloves slap leather gloves. Leather gloves slap glass. Leather goods? Leather bads!

Coco Chanel and the Carter Family crawl from the Maze.

V.

V. V. V. V. V. V. V.

V. V. V. V. V. V. V. V. V. V. V. V. V.

V. V. V. V. V. V. V. V. V. V. V. V. V. V. V. V. V. V. V. V. V. V. V. V. V. V. V. V. V. V. V. V. V. V. V. V. V. V. V. V. V. V.

V. V. V. V. V. V. V. V. V. V. V. V. V. V. V. V. V. V. V. V. V. V. V. V. V. V. V. V. V. V. V. V. V. V. V. V. V. V. V. V. V. V. V. V. V. V. V. V. V.

THE NEXT NIGHT . . .

Mirror.

Mirror. Mirror.

Mirror. Mirror. Mirror.

Mirror. Mirror. Mirror. Mirror. Mirror. Mirror. Mirror. Mirror. Mirror. Mirror. Mirror. Mirror. Mirror. Mirror. Mirror.

Elsa Schiaparelli and me in a Mirror Maze.

Sweat, snot, nosebleed blood. Sputum. Mirrors smeared like lab slides. Carrie steps down the corridor. Shadows under her eyes are eye shadow.

"You look like hell," I say.

Pale as powder. "I don't care," Carrie says. "Jimmie, he's—"

"Breathing better? But of course." Schiaparelli licks Carrie's reflection. The mirror smells.

Mirrors have edges. Mirrors age. "He needs more *Shocking!*" Carrie says. "How do I know you'll deliver it? How can I trust you?"

"Sssshhh," Schiaparelli says. "I have already delivered another dose of scent to his Sanitarium. I've also seen to it that your husband is treated by the most respected respirologist in all of Asheville. His name is Dr. Acula."

"He sounds important," Carrie says.

Fangs are lifelike. Schiaparelli smiles.

ii.

Carrie Rodgers.

Carrie Rodgers. Carrie Rodgers.

Carrie Rodgers. Carrie Rodgers. Carrie Rodgers.

Carrie Rodgers. Carrie Rodgers. Carrie Rodgers. Carrie Rodgers. Carrie Rodgers. Carrie Rodgers. Carrie Rodgers. Carrie Rodgers.

Carrie Rodgers and Elsa Schiaparelli and me in a Mirror Maze. Elsa Lanchester plays Elsa Schiaparelli. There's a resemblance.

"Am I late?" Schiaparelli says.

"Fashionably." I kiss her hand. "You smell divine."

"I am divine." She fans herself. "The latest fragrance from *Maison de Schiaparelli*. I call it *Shocking!*—as in freak shows—'shocking and amazing!'"

"How do I look?" Schiaparelli's dress is orange, yellow, and pink. Mostly pink. Sleeves sparkle. Sequins are celluloid. "I cut it from sideshow banners. 'Valentines,' freaks call them. Isn't that quaint?"

"The sequins!" I say. "Superb!"

Screen as swatch:

(((
(((
(((
(((
(((
(((
(((
(((

"Otto is my embroiderer," Schiaparelli says as the camera pans to . . .

Otto, the Octopus Man. He comes down the corridor. An extra arm extends from the center of his chest.

"He sews like he has three hands," she says. "Which he does!"

"Larry is my cutter," Schiaparelli says. Cut to Larry, the Lobster Boy. Claws for hands. He wears a bib.

"Pinny is my draper," she says. Pinny, the Human Pincushion. Pins through his cheeks. Pins through his earlobes. Pinched between his teeth. A stick of French chalk stuck behind his ear. Shears in his hand.

"Pinking shears!" Schiaparelli says.

Violet and Daisy.

Violet and Daisy. Violet and Daisy.

Violet and Daisy. Violet and Daisy. Siamese Twins in a Mirror Maze.

"Violet is my *première main*, my main seamstress," Schiaparelli says. "Daisy is my *seconde main*. Violet takes the mock-up of a dress to Daisy, who distributes it to the sewing staff, who complete the finished garments. Daisy, darling, call them in?"

Freaks file in. From the cast of *Freaks*. A midgetess. A giantess. Fatty, the Fat Lady has an all-day lollipop. She eats three a day. The Bearded Lady braided her beard. To be pretty. A Chicken Lady carries in the Human Worm. The Worm was born without arms, without legs. Born a dress form.

Freaks.

Carrie Rodgers. Freaks.

Carrie Rodgers. Freaks. Carrie Rodgers.

Freaks. Carrie Rodgers. Freaks. Carrie Rodgers. Freaks.

Carrie Rodgers. Freaks. Carrie Rodgers. Freaks. Carrie Rodgers. Freaks. Carrie Rodgers. Freaks.

Carrie Rodgers and Elsa Schiaparelli and freaks and me in a Mirror Maze.

"Who creates clothes for the Human Worm?" Schiaparelli says. "He has to have himself wrapped in burlap.

"Where does Fatty shop? Not in stores. She wouldn't fit in the fitting room. She mail-orders three dresses at a time. A large, a large, and a large. She sews them together and what has she got? A skin-tight tent!

"Does Sears Roebuck have a Freak Boutique? Where does the Half-Man, Half-Woman shop? The ladies' floor? The men's floor? Where do Siamese Twins buy twin sets? Where do they buy a ball gown with four sleeves and two collars? They have to sew their own. Simplicity doesn't print patterns for freaks!

"The Gorilla begs dead monkeys from the circus. Skins them, cures them. Dry cleaners won't touch him. Launderers won't let him in. Freaks—your sad sartorial stories are history. I, Elsa Schiaparelli, the Empress of Satanic Style, the Wicked Witch of the Weft—I will sew your clothes. More than that, I will dress the whole world in your clothes!"

"Dress like us!" Freaks form a ring around Carrie, chanting: "Dress like us! Dress like us! Dress like us!"

"The Carnival Collection!" Schiaparelli says.

Bats beat their way through the Maze. Clutched in their claws: haute couture. Carrie stands on a tailor's stage. She's believably scared.

"The Spidora Dress," Schiaparelli says.

Bats drape a dress over Carrie. Cinderella had birds.

"Spidoras are half women, half spiders," Schiaparelli says. "The dress is crepe printed with cobwebs. Diamanté dew-drops. A celluloid necklace studded with flies. Gold flies. Diamond eyes. Jean Schlumberger for *Maison de Schiaparelli.*"

Bats fly it over to a clothes rack. Bats are hangers.

"The Geek Gown," Schiaparelli says.

Bats bring it over to Carrie. Blood dripping down the collar. "It's not blood," Schiaparelli says. "It's beading. Gore embroidered on the breast. Gores in the skirt.

"The Girl-to-Gorilla Dress," she says.

Bats bring it over. A brown gown trimmed with monkey

fur. "Monkey fur bracelet. Monkey fur boots. Stockings are cheetah-print. How fast do they run?"

Clothes keep coming. "A cape composed of chicken feathers —cape *au coq*—the Chicken Lady! Flesh-tone fabric printed with anchors, angels, roses, and hearts—a tattooist's flash—the Tattooed Lady! A dress with a *trompe l'oeil* pattern—sequined scorch marks—the Electric Girl!

"Mirrors are *trompe l'oeil* to me," she says.

"Scorch marks?" Carrie shakes her head. "Sequins shouldn't be scary. Still, they're so shiny. So sparkly." She feels the fancywork. "So—ouch!"

(((
(((
(((
(((
(((
(((
(((
(((

"Blood?" Schiaparelli licks her lipstick.

"I smell it, too!" I lick my lipstick. Men can wear lipstick in motion pictures.

"Sequins cut me!" Carrie hides her hand behind her back. With her sleeve she tries to wipe blood from embroidery.

((
((
((
((
((
((
((
((

"You bleed on it, you bought it!" Schiaparelli says.

"The only thing better than sequins—bloody sequins!" she says.

"What is your blood type?" She stalks toward Carrie. "Sequins say—'O!'"

"Don't drink me!" Carrie says. "Please!" She stumbles back off the stage. Mirror, mirror on the wall? Mirrors, mirrors are the walls!

Something stops Schiaparelli cold.

"That odious odor!" she says.

"That sickening smell!" she says.

"It's her—Coco Chanel!" she says.

Mirrors reflect mirrors. Carrie reflects forever. Freaks ad infinitum. "Are you certain Chanel's here?" I say. "Wouldn't we see her?"

"I don't need to see her." Schiaparelli sniffs Johnny Eck. "Sweat," she says. Eck walks on his hands. He was born with no legs. No inseam. She sniffs Garvey, the Gorilla from the Girl-to-Gorilla Act. "Gasoline," she says. Fake gorillas soak their suits in gasoline, then soak them in sun.

"What have we here?" Schiaparelli says.

Pointy, pointier, pointier, pointiest—pinheads. A family of four female encephalites. Skulls shaped like dunce caps. Disease deformed them.

"Puzzling." Schiaparelli swirls around them. "Where in the world would pinheads purchase Chanel perfume?" She strokes their pinafores. Pinheadfores? "And where in the world would they find fabric printed with a Sonia Delaunay pattern, from Chanel's collection for Spring?"

"Touché, Elsa," says the pointiest pinhead—Coco Chanel! She pulls off her pinhead. It's rubber. It resembles a breast.

"Curse you, Schiaparelli!" Mother Maybelle says, pulling off her pinhead. "You've got a nose like a pig!"

"Face like a pig," Sara says, pulling off her pinhead.

"They made me wear a dress," A.P. says.

Freaks.

Carrie Rodgers. Freaks.

Coco Chanel. Freaks. The Carter Family.

Freaks. Carrie Rodgers. Freaks. Coco Chanel. Freaks. The Carter Family. Freaks. Carrie Rodgers. Freaks. Coco Chanel. Freaks. The Carter Family. Freaks.

Carrie Rodgers and Coco Chanel and the Carter Family and Elsa Schiaparelli and freaks and me in a Mirror Maze.

"Disguises!" Schiaparelli says.

"How uncharacteristically clever of you, Coco!" she says.

"However did you come up with such a devilish idea?" she says.

"I stole it from you, Elsa," Chanel says. "From you and your flunky." She claps her hands, cueing—"Dr. Acula!"

White hair, white lab coat—the doctor dodders down the corridor, straight from central casting.

"Doctor!" Schiaparelli says.

"I didn't summon you!" she says.

"Leave the Maze, *tout de suite!*" she says.

"Doctor?" Carrie says. "From the Sanitarium?

"How is Jimmie?" She dashes to his side. "Is he better?"

Both she and her brooch are *en tremblant*. "Has he asked after me?"

"*Monsieur le Docteur*," Chanel says, "has been treating *Monsieur* Rodgers at the Sanitarium. Spraying him with *Shocking!* Shocking him with sprayings.

"He might have gone unnoticed," she says. "But he deported himself like no doctor I'd ever seen. Cursing the Red Cross. Drinking from a blood bag.

"He's not a doctor at all!" she says. "He's not even a man!" She grabs a hank of his hair. Rips off his face. It's Lon Chaney! He makes a ghoulish grimace. Phantom of the Opera? Phantom of the Opry! "When I threatened him with *Chanel N°5*," she says, "he buckled. Like a belt!"

Freaks.

Carrie Rodgers. Freaks.

Coco Chanel. Freaks. The Carter Family.

Freaks. Carrie Rodgers. Freaks. Coco Chanel. Freaks. The Carter Family. Freaks. Carrie Rodgers. Freaks. Coco Chanel. Freaks. The Carter Family. Freaks.

Carrie Rodgers and Coco Chanel and the Carter Family and Elsa Schiaparelli and Lon Chaney and freaks and me in a Mirror Maze.

"You?" Carrie picks up Dr. Acula's face. It's rubber, stiff with sweat and spit. The mask has bad breath. "You're my respected respirologist?"

"A demon!" Mother Maybelle says.

"A demon in disguise!" Sara says.

"Look!" A.P. puts on the mask. "I'm Dr. Scary!"

Maybelle swats him. The mask moves. Eyebrows stick out of eye sockets. Who's his optometrist? Meret Oppenheim?

"Renfield, you fool," Schiaparelli says to Chaney, stretching the mask till it snaps. "I told you to tend to *Monsieur*

Rodgers—and you failed. You betrayed me to Chanel and her hayseed stooges. *Et tu,* Brutus? Étui, Brutus?"

Chaney falls to his knees. Mimes misery.

"*Chanel N°5* frightens you?" Schiaparelli says. "What it does to you is nothing compared to what I will do to you. I will have you baptized a Baptist. I will impale you on a wooden steeple. I will tattoo the Old Testament onto your chest. Kill Chanel! Fang her! Feast on her! Or I shall kill you—again!"

Chaney charges Chanel. Chanel sprays him. Perfume films his eyes. He sees sandalwood! He sees ylang-ylang! He sees Lily of the Valley! Chaney concocted the coating—collodion and egg white. She sprays again. He screeches in close-up. He smells like number two. He can't smell. His nose is mortician's wax. It drips down his lips. His jaw drops. Off. The things he does with gutta-percha! She sprays again. His body bursts into flames. Blazing blue. Fifth-degree burns. He runs around. *No Running*, a sign says. Mirror Mazes don't have fire exits. Heat blackens mirrors. Heat, age, and bats. Mirrors ripple like they've been marcelled. Like laughing mirrors. From Funhouses.

Smoke.

Carrie Rodgers. Smoke.

Coco Chanel. Freaks. Smoke.

Freaks. Smoke. Freaks. Coco Chanel. Smoke. The Carter Family. Smoke. Carrie Rodgers. Freaks. Smoke. Freaks. The Carter Family. Smoke.

Carrie Rodgers and Coco Chanel and the Carter Family and Elsa Schiaparelli and freaks and me in a Mirror Maze. Lon Chaney's charred corpse.

"You lied to me," Carrie says to Schiaparelli.

"*Quel dommage*," Schiaparelli says. "Renfield administered doses of *Shocking!* to *Monsieur* Rodgers. *Shocking!* made *Monsieur* breathe better.

"Madame Rodgers, would you rather the *Shocking!* treatment stopped?" she says. "Would you rather he went back to breathing *Chanel N°5?* Would you rather your husband looked like—" She fingers a freak. "Like him?"

The Human Skeleton.

"Skelly," Schiaparelli says. "He used to be a banker."

Skelly's dressed in a diaper.

"He contracted tuberculosis," she says. "It started out in his lungs. It spread." Skelly's skin and bones. Thin as a woman's watch.

"Doctors treated him the best ways they knew how," she says. "Removed a rib. Collapsed a lung. Pierced his lungs with needles, trying in vain to drain sputum." A pattern punched in his chest. Like in wingtips.

"Doctors failed," she says. "As the disease lays waste to his lungs, tissue turns to sponge. With each cough, he doesn't only do damage to himself. He spreads disease through the air—droplets of TB, of tissue, of blood, of pus. He's a putrid perfume bottle—atomizing itself!"

"*Un atomiseur!*" I say.

"*Un atomonsieur!*" Schiaparelli says.

"Dying slowly?" Carrie says. "In strange towns? In a seedy sideshow? Like Mr. Skelly—a laughingstock to be mocked?" She stares at Skelly, then at Schiaparelli. Mists. "I won't let that happen to my husband. I won't. I can't."

"It's a trick!" Maybelle says.

"It's a double-cross!" Sara says.

"Mrs. Spaghetti!" A.P. says. "She'll eat you!"

"Schiaparelli won't save Skelly," Chanel says to Carrie, "and she won't save *Monsieur* Rodgers! She'll turn the two of you into skeletons—human or otherwise!"

"I know," Carrie says, hanging her head. "It's in the script."

She steps up onto the tailor's stage.

"The Human Skeleton Dress," Schiaparelli says.

Bats beat down the corridor. Drape Carrie in a black jersey.

"Skelly inspired this ensemble," Schiaparelli says. "I'm sure, Madame Rodgers, that you can carry it with a certain *élan.*"

Clavicles, scapulae, spine—Carrie caresses bones. Soft bones. The dress has a skeleton. The dress has TB. Bones are embroideries. Raised ridges sewn onto the cloth. A technique called trapunto. Ribs on the bodice. Collarbones on the collar.

"And you thought corsets had boning." Schiaparelli pins the dress to Carrie. To her shoulders, her arms, her torso, her waist. Endless needles. Steel through skin. Carrie gasps.

Black hides blood. Blood soaks her. Trapunto bones absorb it. The bones are stuffed with batting. Schiaparelli licks blood from her own fingers. "Blood," she says, "tastes like pins!"

"The Fortune Teller's turban!" Schiaparelli says. "The Witch Doctor's skull stick! The Ubangi's lip plate! The Snake Lady—her anaconda is a boa! The Alligator Man—what a purse he would make!

"Freak fashion," she says. "Geek chic. It inspired my new haute couture collection for humans—the Carnival Collection! Soon Schiaparelli clients will dress like the Half-Man, Half-Woman and the Mule-Faced Lady. Ostrich girls in ostrich plumes. Lobster ladies in lobster gowns.

"It's like I always say: Clothes make the inhuman."

"Smell!" Schiaparelli sprays *Shocking!* Sprays herself. Perfume clings to dead skin. It smells pink. "The top note—sugar." Pink popcorn, pink cotton candy, pink bubble gum. "The middle note—sawdust." Pink sawdust.

"The bottom?" Chanel says.

"Blood!" Schiaparelli says, spraying. "The blood of little boys, the blood of little girls. A bead in every bottle." She sprays. "To the living, it's undetectable. To the undead, it's delectable." She sprays. "From miles away, we can smell it, we can follow it, we can find the women who wear it. The women who wear it, the men they're with—" She sprays Chanel. "And you!"

"Which perfume do witches wear?" I say.
"*Brumes!*" Schiaparelli says. "By Coty!"
"Which perfume do werewolves wear?"
"*Flèches!*" she says. "By Lancôme!"

"Fragrance and fashion are only the beginning," Schiaparelli says. "I will create carnival cosmetics in kewpie colors. Pink lipsticks. Green rouge. Yellow mascara. Compacts like little Mirror Mazes for makeup.

"Brass rings as earrings," she says. "Dangling earrings shaped like that silly ride, The Swings. Do you know it? Children sit in chairs suspended from chains. When the ride spins, the chairs fly. It's a chandelier. Children are teardrops.

"Wigs in pink and blue, like cotton candy," she says. "Furs in pink and blue, like cotton candy, and glazed like candy apples. Silk scarves printed with glowing eyeballs, the sort one sees painted on the walls in a Haunted House. Capes trimmed with foxtails. Carnies staple tails to the walls of Haunted Houses."

"Who's afraid of foxtails?" I say.

"Foxes!" Schiaparelli says.

"Haute couture?" Schiaparelli says. "*Haute horreur!*"

"Department stores in downtowns across the country," she says, "will sprinkle the aisles with pink sawdust.

"Mirrors on columns, mirrors on counters," she says. "Why do department store perfume departments have so many mirrors? I will make them into Mazes.

"Do you know what a factice is?" she says. "A promotional perfume bottle. I will create factices of *Shocking!* that stand two stories tall. Department store customers can step inside them. See the world as perfume sees it. It will be a ride!

"Escalators I'll cover with boards," she says. "Customers can slide down them as they do Funhouse chutes. The slide will burn holes in their trousers and skirts and hose. They'll have to buy new ones—from me!

"Tightrope walkers will walk from floor to floor, across

first-floor courts, over the counters of Cosmetics and Notions. Acrobats will dangle from ceilings, contorting. Elevator cages will contain lions and tigers and dancing bears.

"Valentines will fly over Fifth Avenue," she says. "Store show windows will feature freaks. Mannequins with three arms, mannequins with no legs. Female forms fitted with heads from male mannequins. Department stores will be sideshows. Saks, Bergdorf Goodman, and Henri Bendel. Bullock's in Los Angeles. Neiman Marcus in Dallas. Wanamaker's in Philadelphia. Marshall Field's in Chicago."

"Lord & Taylor?" I say.

"Bite your tongue!" Schiaparelli says.

"When all the world's well-dressed women are dressed and perfumed like freaks," Schiaparelli says, "I will make them freaks—in a carnival, a vampire carnival—a carnival of fashion and death!" She changes. Fangs flower. Pupils as pink paillettes. "And freaks are only part of the fun!

"Men will be rides.

"Women will be games.

"Children will be snacks."

Schiaparelli's face is a special effect.

"Mr. Carter," Schiaparelli says. "I see you staring at my sequins." Beneath her sequins: shadows of sequins. "Would you like to stroke them?"

"So shiny!" A.P. says.

"So sparkly!" Spellbound, he shuffles toward her. "So . . ."

"So stupid!" Maybelle wallops him with her shoe. Plow shoe. The sole's wood. Leather's oak-tanned. Supple as steel. "What are you—French?"

"Dear Jesus," Maybelle says.

"Holy Father in Heaven," Sara says.

"Ow." A.P.'s bruises are coming up blue.

"Thank you for saving your stupid son, A.P." Maybelle and kin drop to their knees in the Mirror Maze. "Mrs. Schiaparelli seduced him with sequins. Shininess is a sin. Satan is satin. Country music is for plain folks. Help him be plain. Help him be navy, gray, or black. Maybe brown. Amen."

"Prayers can't protect you from my paillettes!" Schiaparelli says. "Ecru is not a cure! My sequins are sirens—rich, radiant, ravishing—"

"Evil!" Chanel says.

"Your sequins are evil!" she says.

"It's not melodramatics!" She crosses to where bats clutch the Carnival Collection. When she sprays *Chanel N°5* on the Electric Girl Dress—

Bang! Bang! Bang!—spangles spark. "Holy water destroys them," she says. *Bang! Bang! Bang!*—spangles blister, then burn. Scorching scorch marks. "Christian sequins would not be charred by *Chanel N°5!*"

Otto shakes his fists at her. Fist. Fist. Fist.

"What's the secret of your sequins, Elsa?" Chanel says. "What makes them as volatile as vampires?"

"They are vampires," Schiaparelli says.

Wind whips up.

"Sequins, *c'est moi!*" Schiaparelli says, floating off the floor.

Thunder! Lightning! Chanel's blown off balance. A.P. clings to Sara, who clings to Maybelle. Maybelle's dress clings to her like it's a Vionnet. It's not.

"I make them," Schiaparelli says. "And they make me!"

How to make movie thunder—shake an X-ray. How to make movie lightning—flick lights on and off.

"They're in my veins!" Schiaparelli smashes a mirror with her fist. What's bad luck to a vampire? What's seven years? With a sliver of silver she slits her wrist. Glitter gushes out. "I'm the *Vogue* vampire. I don't have blood—I have embellishments!"

"Sequins!" she says.

((
((
((
((
((
((
(((
((

"Beads!" she says.

●●

●●

●●

●●

●●

●●

●●

●●

"Crystals!" she says.

****

****

****

****

****

****

****

****

Le sang by Lesage! Fancies flow from Schiaparelli, then blow through the Maze. Whirling like weather in the wind. The forecast—frou-frou.

"I can't see!" Maybelle says.

"I see sequins!" Sara says.

"Srgmmmffft!" A.P.'s mouth full of frippery.

"*Ciel*!" Chanel says. Sequins sting like sand. Crystals cut like ice. Blown beads embed skin like BB's. She feels her way forward. Is that a bat, or a floater? Is the mirror chipped, or is she seeing things? Is that sweat sliding down her skin, or blood? Coco Chanel and the Carter Family crawl from the Maze.

Blood seeps out in cc's.

●●●●●((((*****●●●●●((((*****●●●●●((((*****●●●●●((
((*****●●●●●((((*****●●●●●((((*****●●●●●((((*****●
●●●●((((*****●●●●●((((*****●●●●●((((*****●●●●●(((
(*****●●●●●((((*****●●●●●((((*****●●●●●((((*****●
●●●●((((*****●●●●●((((*****●●●●●((((*****●●●●●(((
(*****●●●●●((((*****●●●●●((((*****●●●●●((((*****●
●●●●((((*****●●●●●((((*****●●●●●((((*****●●●●●(((
(*****●●●●●((((*****●●●●●((((*****●●●●●((((*****

THE NEXT NIGHT . . .

Carrie Rodgers.

Carrie Rodgers. Carrie Rodgers.

Carrie Rodgers. Carrie Rodgers. Carrie Rodgers.

Carrie Rodgers. Carrie Rodgers. Carrie Rodgers. Carrie Rodgers. Carrie Rodgers. Carrie Rodgers. Carrie Rodgers. Carrie Rodgers.

Carrie Rodgers and Elsa Schiaparelli and me in a Mirror Maze.

"A present." Schiaparelli hands her a doll.

"A kewpie?" Carrie says. Plaster of Paris. Painted black. It's bumpy: the doll's bones bulge from her body. Ribs in relief.

"A kewpie of you," Schiaparelli says. "You in your costume—the Human Skeleton Dress." The doll's face is airbrushed on. Glitter rouges cheeks and lips. There's a slot in her skull. Schiaparelli slips in a penny.

It rattles in the doll like TB.

"Why?" Carrie says.

"You're the star of my carnival," Schiaparelli says. "When

it's over, fans will have a souvenir—a memento of you."

"And me?" Carrie turns the doll upside down. Scratched into the base: *Southern Statuary*. Statuary companies make dolls as a sideline. Tombstones pay the bills. "What will happen to me when the carnival ends?"

"I'll devour you." Schiaparelli brushes back Carrie's hair. "Tonight, a taste." Fangs flash. She bites her neck. Carrie can't speak. She drops the doll. Sound effect. Schiaparelli steps back so the camera can capture: nail polish leaking from her lips. On Carrie's neck: scarlet sequins.

3

i.

"Carnivals!" Schiaparelli says.

"Calliopes and carousels!" she says.

"Cute kewpie dolls!" she says. "And candy!

"Children love it all," she says. "Vampires love children."

Carrie Rodgers.

Carrie Rodgers. Carrie Rodgers.

Carrie Rodgers. Carrie Rodgers. Carrie Rodgers.

Carrie Rodgers. Carrie Rodgers. Carrie Rodgers. Carrie Rodgers. Carrie Rodgers. Carrie Rodgers. Carrie Rodgers. Carrie Rodgers.

Carrie Rodgers and Elsa Schiaparelli and me in a Mirror Maze.

"At my vampire carnival, the gent at the Guess Your Age game will guess your age within a hundred years—or you win a prize!

"At my vampire carnival, I will not give away goldfish. Play the Fish Pond and win—a baby! Play the Milk Bottle Toss and win—a baby! Boy babies, girl babies, arranged on prize racks, screaming their lovely lungs out!"

"At my vampire carnival, I'll pinken popcorn with baby blood. Snow cones will come in a single flavor—baby blood. Babies stretched from taffy hooks.

"At my vampire carnival, when you play the Baby Rack, you won't have to pitch baseballs at stuffed dolls. Pitch them at real babies. Break them! Bust them! Pulverize them like plates! Floating in the Fish Pond—dead babies. Corpses puffy like soufflés.

"At my vampire carnival, prizes will be dolls—dead babies stuffed with sawdust. Dead babies will dangle from bamboo canes. Pillows will be babies stuffed and stitched with sayings: *Home Sweet Home. Mother Knows Best.*"

"At my vampire carnival, candy apples will be candy babies. Hot dogs stuffed with stillborns. Baby hamburgers. Baby back ribs. Bar-b-que? Baby-que!

"At my vampire carnival, when you pitch balls at the Dip, a baby will drop into a tank of water and drown. When you swing the hammer at the Test Your Strength game, a baby flies up the rope. If it rings the bell, you win!

"At my vampire carnival, you'll win balloons made of babies—soft skin stretched out and stitched shut and blown full of air. That balloon has eyebrows! At my
vampire carnival, the wax museum will feature babies—babies who died being dipped into barrels of molten wax. Frozen forever!"

"At my vampire carnival, buy bubble gum made from a baby's tongue. Root beer! My secret ingredients are sassafras, nutmeg—and baby!

"At my vampire carnival, Shooting Gallery guns will bear real bullets. The targets will be babies. *BB's pour les bébés*. At the Knife Throw, you'll throw knives at babies strapped to a board. Win the one you wound! Drink it there or take it home! Sawdust soaks up blood. Blood makes it hard as wood.

"At my vampire carnival, the torture exhibit will put the 'die' in 'dioramas.' All the familiar favorites—the Iron Maiden, the Chinese Water Torture, the Rat Cage, the Rack. The tortured will be babies—living babies! The Funhouse will be fun. Try walking over a pit of squirming, squalling babies—now that's a Turkey Trot!"

"At my vampire carnival, you'll see pickled babies at the freak show. Real babies, wrested from the womb and drowned in jars of chloroform.

"At my vampire carnival, freaks will be babies—babies I infected with tuberculosis. With smallpox. With wounds that go gangrenous. The hues! Some with ichthyosis, so their skin scales like they're lizards. Some I'll poison with silver nitrate, so their skin turns a pretty purple.

"At my vampire carnival, the Mirror Maze's mirrors will be printed with pictures of movie stars. At my vampire carnival, the Haunted House will be haunted. Babies dressed as priests and nuns! Baby Jesus in a bed of hay! God himself will drop down from a trap door. A Salvation Army suit stuffed with sawdust. A second-hand scarecrow. God is my pincushion!

"At my vampire carnival, a sign in the sideshow will say, *Baby Rattler.* Beneath it, a cage containing a baby and a rattlesnake. Live baby. Live snake. How colorfully that child will cry! How colorfully that child will die!

"At my vampire carnival, you'll see chimeras in the freak show—bird wings sewn to a live baby's back. Bird beaks sewn to a live baby's lips. The pelt of a baby stoat sewn to a live baby's skin. The babies will be alive for a little while.

"At my vampire carnival, you'll ride real carousel ponies—rotting carcasses speared on poles, like dress forms! You won't grab for a brass ring—but for a baby! At my vampire carnival, babies decked out with bullwhips and jodhpurs will star in the live animal show. Three lions and a baby. Three tigers and a baby. Hyenas. Hilarious! Babies will ride on horseback. Till they're tossed and trampled. I'll shoot babies from a cannon. Spray the audience with snacks. At my vampire carnival, there'll be no wooden stakes—tents will be tacked down with dead babies!"

"Beast!" Carrie shrieks. "Babies are beautiful! Why do you—" Grabbing her guts, she stumbles off the tailor's stage. "I—I—feel sick!"

"Of course you do," Schiaparelli says. "You're in a

motherly way!" She cackles. "It's true, Madame! I tasted it in your blood—another being's blood. A baby boy!"

"I—I'm going to have a son?" Carrie says.

"Yes," Schiaparelli says. "Then I'll have him—for supper!"

ii.

Mirror.

Mirror. Mirror.

Mirror. Mirror. Mirror.

Mirror. Mirror. Mirror. Mirror. Mirror. Mirror. Mirror. Mirror. Mirror. Mirror. Mirror. Mirror. Mirror. Mirror. Mirror.

Elsa Schiaparelli in a Mirror Maze.

Sweat, snot, nosebleed blood. Sputum. Mirrors smeared like lab slides. Carrie steps down the corridor. Shadows under her eyes are eye shadow.

"You look like hell," Schiaparelli says.

Pale as powder. "I don't care," Carrie says. "Jimmie, he's—"

"Still breathing better? But of course." Schiaparelli licks Carrie's reflection. The mirror smells.

Mirrors have edges. Mirrors age. "I must speak to him," Carrie says.

"Sssshhh," Schiaparelli says. "Be calm—you have a boy to

bear. I want him to be the picture of health—bouncing, beautiful. Bloody."

"Jimmie wanted a baby so badly," Carrie says. "A son to carry on his name. He never dreamed it would happen, not with . . . not with his health." She clutches Schiaparelli's collar. "Please, Mrs. Schiaparelli, let my son live. Let Jimmie have him. I already gave you my body and soul. I don't know what else I can give."

"Mrs. Schiaparelli?"

Schiaparelli stands Carrie on the tailor's stage.

"Mrs. Schiaparelli, what are you doing?"

Schiaparelli slips off Carrie's coat. Unbuttons her bodice. Unbuttons her brassiere. She licks a nipple. She pinches a nipple.

Carrie gasps. In the mirrors, she's all alone.

Schiaparelli kneels on the stage. She lifts Carrie's skirt, hides her head beneath. Licking panties like it's pink lace she likes. Panties slide down. Schiaparelli claws Carrie's ass crack. Pink fingernails in pink flesh. Carrie's cunt wets Schiaparelli's tongue. Red, red, red—her cunt's Elizabeth Arden red.

Mirror.

Mirror. Mirror.

Mirror. Mirror. Mirror.

Mirror. Mirror. Mirror. Mirror. Mirror. Mirror. Mirror. Mirror. Mirror. Mirror. Mirror. Mirror. Mirror. Mirror. Mirror.

Me in a Mirror Maze.

Sweat, snot, nosebleed blood. Sputum. Mirrors smeared like lab slides. Jimmie steps down the corridor. He's looking hale and handsome. Matinée idol material. I've never seen a matinée.

"You look delicious," I say.

"Not so fast." He tosses sawdust on the floor.

"What's this?" I say. "A hillbilly jigsaw puzzle?"

"Sawdust," he says. "I read all about vampires. You have to count every shred. It's your compulsion." He tosses beans. "Count these, too."

Hillbilly bubble bath.

Mirrors have edges. Mirrors age.

"Beans bedamned," I say, sweeping them aside with my brogue.

"Don't you dare touch me!" he says. "I came for Carrie. I know what she did. She sold her soul so that I could be made whole."

"She will never know you were here," I say. A cracked mirror is atmosphere. The mirror is real. The crack is fake. White wax, cobwebbed. "Too bad, too. Did you know she's with child? Your son will never meet you. I'm going to eat you."

"I can give you money." He holds out a wad. "I can give you gold." He holds out a watch. "There must be something I have that you want."

"Yes," I say. "Your ass."

"You—you're a—you're a queer?" Jimmie says.

"All monsters are queers, *Monsieur* Rodgers," Schiaparelli says, sweeping into the scene.

"Who is able to bring the dead back to life?" she says. "God and the Devil. The Devil makes dead men into monsters: immortal, immoral—and queer. Zombies are queer. Frankenstein's monster was queer. It's fitting."

"How's that?" Jimmie says.

"Monsters must be scary," she says. "What's scarier than

sodomites? Like the dead, sodomites carry disease. Sodomites, like the dead, dwell underground. Sodomites wear cosmetics like they're corpses. Sodomites and dead men—they all smell like shit—and love it! Cemeteries full of fairies. Vampires are the fairiest of all."

"But Dracula!" Jimmie says.

"Mina Harker meant nothing to the Count," she says. "Nor did Lucy Westenra. Dracula would never drink a woman's blood. He'd rather eat rats. He loved Jonathan. Gilles de Rais? Gay. What do you think Vlad the Impaler impaled? Vampires are dandies. The lavender dead. They love fashion, fragrance, films. Vampires have private lives like silent movie stars. Hays Code? Ha!"

"*Monsieur* Rodgers," Schiaparelli says. "Mr. McCormack could fuck you while you're dead. He could fuck you while you're undead. He could fuck you while you're alive. Whichever way you cut it, you'll be fucked. What will it be?"

She turns into vapor. Vanishes.

"Our Father . . . " Jimmie says.

I stand him on the tailor's stage.

"Who art in Heaven, hallowed be thy name."

I slip off his coat. Slip off his shirt. Slip off his undershirt. I lick a nipple. Lick an underarm. It looks like it needs ironing. Creases. Curly hair. I taste bacteria.

"Thy Kingdom come—thy Kingdom—oh, God, that tickles!"

I kneel on the stage. Unbuckle his belt. Tug down his trousers. I lick his underpants like it's cotton I crave. Underpants drop. I pull on his penis. It bloats like a corpse. It tastes like pennies. Slit big as a kewpie's coin slot.

Carrie Rodgers.

Carrie Rodgers. Carrie Rodgers.

Carrie Rodgers. Carrie Rodgers. Carrie Rodgers.

Carrie Rodgers. Carrie Rodgers. Carrie Rodgers. Carrie Rodgers. Carrie Rodgers. Carrie Rodgers. Carrie Rodgers. Carrie Rodgers.

Carrie Rodgers in a Mirror Maze.

"Darling?" Jimmie says.

"Darling!" She dashes into his arms.

"What did that monster do to you?" he says.

"I'm not sick—my dress is." The Human Skeleton Dress. Choker of carnival glass. "Jimmie, I thought I'd never hold you again!"

"I missed you." He kisses her. "I need you." He kneels. Draws up her dress. Draws down her drawers. Flicks his tongue into the folds of her cunt. Fingers in fur. Fingers slide into her hole. Pinkie finger. Ring finger. It's like he's sizing himself for a ring.

"God!" she gasps. Grabs his hair. His head slides off in her hands. A mask. It's not Jimmie—it's Jimmy Cagney! She screams. Grabs his hair. Jimmy's head slides off in her hands. It's not Jimmy Cagney—it's Gary Cooper! It's not Gary Cooper—it's Wallace Beery! Clark Gable! Will Rogers!

Will's mask comes off.

It's Schiaparelli.

Jimmie Rodgers.

Jimmie Rodgers. Jimmie Rodgers.

Jimmie Rodgers. Jimmie Rodgers. Jimmie Rodgers.

Jimmie Rodgers. Jimmie Rodgers. Jimmie Rodgers. Jimmie

Rodgers. Jimmie Rodgers. Jimmie Rodgers. Jimmie Rodgers. Jimmie Rodgers.

Jimmie Rodgers in a Mirror Maze.

"Darling?" Carrie says.

"Darling!" He dashes into her arms.

"What did that monster do to you?" she says.

"*Shocking!* saved me—but what price did I pay?" He has his color back. "Carrie, I thought I'd never hold you again!"

"I missed you." She kisses him. "I need you." Unbuckling his belt, she pulls down his pants. His drawers. His cock's crimson. She licks its length. Thread veins. Varicose veins. Veins like piping up his penis. She licks his balls, the seam on the underside.

"Carrie!" he says. "What's gotten into you?"

"Your ass," she says, spinning him around. "It's astonishing." His ass—a vaseline shot. She slaps his cheeks. Pulls them apart. His hole's a drawstring drawn up. She licks it. Licks until it smells like spit. Fingers slide inside. Pinkie finger. Ring finger. It's like she's sizing herself for a ring.

"God!" he gasps. Grabs her hair. Her head slides off in his hands. A mask. It's not Carrie—it's Hedy Lamarr! He screams. Grabs her hair. Hedy's head slides off in his hands.

It's not Hedy Lamarr—it's Carole Lombard! It's not Carole Lombard—it's Claudette Colbert! Marlene Dietrich! Norma Shearer!

Norma's mask comes off.

It's me. Fingers slick with oil, sweat, and shit.

"*Parfum glacé!*" I say, smearing it behind my ears.

iii.

Black.

Black. Black.

Black. Black. Black.

Black. Black. Black. Black. Black. Black. Black. Black. Black. Black. Black. Black. Black. Black. Black. Black. Black. Black. Black. Black.

Jimmie Rodgers in a blindfold in a Mirror Maze.

Jimmie tears off his blindfold.

"Surprise!" I'm holding a suit.

"That's the surprise?" he says. "A suit?"

"There are garments that Madame Schiaparelli rarely deigns to design," I say. "Daywear for women. And menswear." The suit's pink. I'm wearing the same suit. I'm as peaked as my lapels. "Put it on."

Jimmie Rodgers.

Jimmie Rodgers. Jimmie Rodgers.

Jimmie Rodgers. Jimmie Rodgers. Jimmie Rodgers.

Jimmie Rodgers. Jimmie Rodgers. Jimmie Rodgers. Jimmie Rodgers. Jimmie Rodgers. Jimmie Rodgers. Jimmie Rodgers. Jimmie Rodgers.

Jimmie Rodgers and me in a Mirror Maze.

Jimmie poses like he's shooting publicity. Blazer buttoned, blazer unbuttoned—he tries it both ways. Plumps his pink pocket puff. Picks pink lint from lapels.

"Pink is your color," I say.

"Pink is for perverts." Jimmie tosses his jacket to the floor. The label on the lining: *Schiaparelli de Paris*. "I won't wear it."

"You will wear what Madame wants you to wear." I leer like Tillie, the Coney Island mascot. "Madame sewed us these suits as a gift. A wedding gift."

"Wedding?" Jimmie says.

"*Oui*." I sniff my boutonnière. It's black. It's silk. "Madame Schiaparelli has decided that you and I will be wed in a Satanic ceremony."

"What the hell are you talking about?" he says.

"In Hell," I say, "men marry men, and women wed

women. In the eyes of God, you're married to Mrs. Rodgers. In the eyes of Beelzebub, you're a bachelor. But not for much longer." I bat my eyelashes. What do you call a pervert vampire in makeup? Mascary! "I'm about to be your bride." I hold out my hand. A ring flashes on my finger. The stone's carnival glass cut like a garnet.

"Your ass is a diamond," I say. "A *chaton*."

Jimmie Rodgers.

Jimmie Rodgers. Jimmie Rodgers.

Jimmie Rodgers. Jimmie Rodgers. Jimmie Rodgers.

Jimmie Rodgers. Jimmie Rodgers. Jimmie Rodgers. Jimmie Rodgers. Jimmie Rodgers. Jimmie Rodgers. Jimmie Rodgers. Jimmie Rodgers.

Jimmie Rodgers and Elsa Schiaparelli and me in a Mirror Maze.

"*La chappelle de Schiaparelli!*" Schiaparelli says.

"A wedding chapel in a Mirror Maze!" she says.

"A wedding chapel," she says, "in a wedding chapel in a wedding chapel in a wedding chapel in a wedding chapel in a wedding chapel!"

"A Mirror Maze has nothing to do with marriage!"

Jimmie says. "Marriage is a sacred ceremony in a church. It's about making a commitment before God. It's about a man and a woman. It's about children. It's about love."

"I love your ass," I say.

"Normals marry normals," Schiaparelli says. "Freaks marry freaks. When freaks marry normals, the whole world goes wild. General Tom Thumb and Lavinia. Chang and Eng, the Siamese Twins, and their brides, the Yates Sisters. Barnum was brilliant—but I am more brilliant. At my vampire carnival, the undead will wed the living!"

"I, too, am to be wed, *Monsieur* Rodgers," Schiaparelli says, sashaying up to him. "My fiancée is beautiful, bright—and her blood tastes like Burgundy."

"*Chérie?*" Schiaparelli says.

Here comes the bride, all dressed in white... Calliope music creeps in from the carnival. Carrie comes down the corridor. Crying.

"Something old, something new, something borrowed, something pink," Schiaparelli says. Carrie's all dressed in pink. A pink dress. A pink mink. Earrings are black elephants, the kind printed on cartons of pink popcorn.

"Through thick and thin," Schiaparelli says, "in sickness and health, in good times, as in bad, she was yours. In a few moments, *Monsieur* Rodgers, she'll be mine."

"Never!" Jimmie charges at Schiaparelli. I trip him. He flies headfirst into a mirror. Splintering it.

Carrie cries out.

"Madame Carrie Schiaparelli—a singsong sound, *n'est-ce pas?*" Schiaparelli bites a bit of broken mirror. How to make a movie mirror: bake sugar into a sheet, glaze it to look like glass. She's chewing the scenery! "Every mirror has a silver lining, *Monsieur* Rodgers. I've decided to name your baby 'Jimmie, Jr.' Sweet, yes? A baby bonbon. I'll devour him *à la mode*."

"Welcome my wedding party!" Schiaparelli says.

"Party?" Jimmie says. "That's Pinny, from the freak show. And Terry, the Tattooed Lady. And Jean, the Half-Man, Half-Woman."

"Terry is my flower girl," Schiaparelli says. Terry has roses tattooed up her arms. Sawdust is confetti. Terry tosses it. It's dyed pink.

"Pinny is my ring bearer," Schiaparelli says. Pinny has rings through his ears, nose, lips, cheeks. "Jean is the maid of honor. And the best man." Pinny tosses pink sawdust. It's cured, not shaved.

Freaks file in. From the cast of *Freaks*. A midgetess. A giantess. Fatty the Fat Lady has an all-day lollipop. She eats three a day. The Bearded Lady braided her beard. To be pretty. The Fire Breather breathes fire. His blazer is asbestos. A Chicken Lady carries in the Human Worm. The Worm was born without arms, without legs. He's wrapped in burlap. He resembles the stogie he's sucking.

"Freaks!" Jimmie says.

"God made you hideously ugly, but He loves you!" he says.

"Why are you helping these vampires?" he says. "They're vile! They're vermin! You're better than this! We can beat them!"

"Freaks are sick," Schiaparelli says. "Sick of you normals. Sick of listening to you, sick of looking at you, sick of lusting after you. Mostly, freaks are sick of looking at themselves—at their own monstrousness. I have made the freaks a vow—to transform them into fashion plates. And more—to transform them into vampires. To make them immune to their ultimate enemy—the mirror!"

"No more mirrors!" Freaks chant. Freaks clap hands.

Paws. Claws. Flippers. Fins. Stumps. "No more mirrors! No more mirrors!"

"The unreflected life is worth living!" Schiaparelli says.

Gypsy scarves, gypsy skirt, gypsy coins—a gypsy, played by character actress Mario Ouspenskaya, comes down the corridor.

"Mandala!" Schiaparelli says.

"At your command," Mandala says in her Romanian or Hungarian accent.

"Mandala, meet Carrie Rodgers," Schiaparelli says. "Carrie, Mandala. Carrie is my bride to be. Mandala is a fortune teller on the midway. She's also Satan's priestess. Who says divination isn't a sin?"

"Dearly deformed," Mandala says, standing on the tailor's stage. "We are gathered here tonight to unite this demon and this damsel in the bonds of macabre matrimony." She laughs. A silver tooth is a laughing mirror. "Should any man or oddity have any reason why Madame Schiaparelli and Madame Rodgers should not be married, speak now or forever hold your peace!"

I have my hand over Jimmie's mouth.

"Where's Chanel when you need her?" Schiaparelli says to Carrie.

Freaks.

Carrie Rodgers. Freaks.

Jimmie Rodgers. Freaks. Carrie Rodgers.

Freaks. Jimmie Rodgers. Freaks. Carrie Rodgers. Freaks. Jimmie Rodgers. Freaks. Carrie Rodgers. Freaks. Jimmie Rodgers. Freaks. Carrie Rodgers. Freaks.

Jimmie Rodgers and Carrie Rodgers and Elsa Schiaparelli and freaks and me in a Mirror Maze.

Freaks.

Carrie Rodgers. Freaks.

Jimmie Rodgers. Freaks. Carrie Rodgers.

Freaks. Jimmie Rodgers. Freaks. Carrie Rodgers. Freaks. Jimmie Rodgers. Freaks. Carrie Rodgers. Freaks. Jimmie Rodgers. Freaks. Carrie Rodgers. Freaks.

Jimmie Rodgers and Carrie Rodgers and Coco Chanel and the Carter Family and Elsa Schiaparelli and freaks and me in a Mirror Maze.

"Satan!" Mandala says.

"Lord of Vermin!" she says. "Monarch of Hell!

"Beelzebub, bring us evil!" she says. "Bring us bile! Bestow your black blessings upon this ceremony!"

A crystal ball. She holds it above her head. Summoning something. A speck. A black speck. Like a fly in a fake ice cube. A bat beats its wings. Grows bigger and bigger, blacker and blacker—and burning? The bat bursts into flames. It squeals. Careens uncontrollably around the crystal ball. Satan is flappable.

"Satan!" Mandala drops the ball. It cracks. A million crystal crumbs. "Something stopped him!" She gasps. "God is in the Maze!"

Crystal balls—rhinestones waiting to happen.

"I am Elsa Schiaparelli!" Schiaparelli says.

"God does not daunt me!" she says. "Good does not daunt me!

"I will wed this woman!" she says. "The honeymoon will be hair-raising!"

"Madame Schiaparelli." Mandala takes her hand. "Do you take this woman, Carrie Rodgers, to be your wife, until you murder her or become bored of her?"

"I . . ." Schiaparelli doesn't say "do." She shrieks, staggers across the sound stage. Face hidden in hands. Scarlet sequins bleed from between fingers.

"Surprise!" Silver snood, silver slippers, silver gloves—Chanel materializes in the middle of the Maze. Ensemble slathered with silver sequins. She bleeds into mirrors. Vice versa. She carries a full flaçon: *Chanel N°5*. "It's called camouflage," she says. "In order to steal into a Mirror Maze, I dressed as a Mirror Maze."

She sprays Schiaparelli. Schiaparelli's skin and flesh burns to bone. Sequins gush from sockets where eyes were.

Mirrors! The Carter Family clatters down the corridor, mirrors tied to suits. Tied, taped, and safety-pinned. Compact mirrors, pocket mirrors, purse mirrors. Squares of silver foil. Mirror-colored.

"Did you get her?" Mother Maybelle says.

"Is she dead?" Sara says.

"Is it safe?" A.P. says.

"Almost." Chanel stands over a cowering Schiaparelli. "Sequins betrayed you, Elsa," she says. "Sequins are mirrors.

Mirrors with holes." She sprays. Schiaparelli's a skull. The Masque of the Pink Death!

"I should have been able to smell you!" Schiaparelli's skull says.

"*Chanel N°5?*" Chanel says.

"I didn't dare wear it," she says. "I wore a new scent.

"The top note—sugar," she says. "Smells pink. Pink popcorn, pink cotton candy. Midway pinks mingling in a Mirror Maze. Sounds nice, *non?*

"The middle note is glass. Blended with the tinctures of silver, steel, and lead crystal. I put in sweat, snot, nosebleed blood. A sample of sputum. I secretly swabbed it during your fashion show. Your defiled *défilé*. I added a drop of vinegar. Carnies clean Mirror Mazes with it, Elsa. Did you know?

"The base note is woodsy. The wood of these floorboards. I decocted the odor, down to the dust, the spilled soda, the bubble gum grafted like skin to pine. Shoe leather from Sears. A soupçon of sawdust. A splash of pine oil. Did you know you must never wax the floor of a Mirror Maze, Elsa? It's dangerous.

"Do you see what I did, Elsa? I extracted the essence of Mirror Maze. I am the Maze. The Maze is mine."

"I am perfume!" Schiaparelli's skull says. "*Parfum du parfum!* The Mirror Maze is my flaçon! My Baccarat bottle! You are the flaw! Humans are flaws!"

Chanel sprays her.

Schiaparelli disappears. A swirl of pink smoke.

"You murdered Madame." I'm lit in the creepiest colors, yellow and red. "You have not killed her style. I will carry on her work. I will lay down my pen and pick up the needle. I will sew clothes for stars like you, Mr. Rodgers. I will dress country stars in freak couture—fine fabrics in carnival colors, festooned with rhinestones, crystals, and beads. I will marry haute couture to hillbilly music—and I will spread the disease of sodomy! For I have found that nothing in this world tastes better than the asses of Country-and-Western stars—nothing!" *Poof!*—I disappear.

"He disappeared!" Maybelle says.

"Disappeared in a poof!" Sara says.

"That seems appropriate," Chanel says.

Chanel and Maybelle and Sara laugh a lot.

"I don't get it," A.P. says. "What's the big joke?"

Jimmie Rodgers.

Carrie Rodgers. Jimmie Rodgers.

Carrie Rodgers. Jimmie Rodgers. Carrie Rodgers.

Jimmie Rodgers. Carrie Rodgers. Jimmie Rodgers. Carrie Rodgers. Jimmie Rodgers. Carrie Rodgers. Jimmie Rodgers. Carrie Rodgers.

Jimmie Rodgers and Carrie Rodgers in a Mirror Maze.

Sunlight streams into the Maze.

"I love you," Jimmie says.

"I love you," Carrie says, resting her head on his shoulder pad.

"Let's go," he says. "Let's eat candy apples. Let's play the Red Wheel. Let's ride the rides—I hear the Tunnel of Love is romantic." He kisses her. "We're alive. Alive at a carnival! I can sing again!"

"Are you sure you're ready?" she says, touching the swell in her stomach.

"Ready as—" He coughs. "Ready as I'll ever—" Coughs. Coughs. Coughs. A stitch in his stomach. He can't stand up straight. "It's nothing," he says, doubling over against glass. "A tickle. A little tickle."

"TB," Carrie says.

"I'm fine." He's lying at her feet.

"It's back." She sinks down beside him. His sleeve's sopping. Sputum. It will dry stiffer than starch. "Without Schiaparelli's satanic perfume, the carnival will kill you," she says. "You have to leave. You have to return to the Sanitarium."

"So they can what—slice me up?" he says. "Stab me with syringes? Shut me in a room to rot?" He coughs. "I'm Jimmie Rodgers! The carnival singer! Who would I be if I stopped—" He hacks. Hemorrhages. Blood and bits of bat shit.

"Jimmie?" She holds his head. "Don't leave me!"

Jimmie burbles. Blood puddles. A red clown shoe on the floor.

"We'll go to Coney Island." Carrie weeps. "We'll ride the roller coasters. The Cyclone. The Tornado. The sea air will do you good. We'll go to Ocean Pier Park. We'll walk the boardwalk. We'll ride the Racing Derby. You can soak up the sun—the California sun. It will cure you. I know it will." Vampires, like perfumes and TB bacteria, decay in daylight. "Jimmie? Jimmie, can you hear me? Say something, Jimmie!"

Jimmie Rodgers.

Carrie Rodgers. Jimmie Rodgers.

Carrie Rodgers. Jimmie Rodgers. Carrie Rodgers.

Jimmie Rodgers. Carrie Rodgers. Jimmie Rodgers. Carrie Rodgers. Jimmie Rodgers. Carrie Rodgers. Jimmie Rodgers.

Jimmie Rodgers and Carrie Rodgers in a Mirror Maze.

Jimmie died.

THE END